for dear Dr Ali

and his wonderful family,

With much admiration
and affection

Riad

THE
DEATH
OF
ALMUSTAFA

THE
DEATH
OF
ALMUSTAFA

RIAD NOURALLAH

With original drawings by
CLARE ALLEN

Quartet Books

First published in 2010 by
Quartet Books Limited
A member of the Namara Group
27 Goodge Street, London W1T 2LD

A catalogue record for this book
is available from the British Library

ISBN   978 0 7043 7211 5

Typeset by Antony Gray
Printed and bound in Great Britain by
T J International Ltd, Padstow, Cornwall

FOR
KAHLIL GIBRAN

(1883-1931)

CONTENTS

DWARF STARS

drifted in the cold eyes that were boring into him, chilling the mesh of his heart.

He shivered, but heaved against the hulking vision, slashing at its horror with the fever of his mind that had created it.

The Stalker retreated, gathering the darkness like a lacerated cloak over his face.

*　　*　　*

It was Nisan, the month of rebirth, and Almustafa was dying. Forty-eight years had passed since he was born on an isle beyond the great sea. There, and though he could not see them, the slopes of his mountain birthplace were flush with the reddest anemones and crowfoots ever seen. It was as if the blood of his heart was ebbing into the blue distance to surge anew through their roots and burn in their petals.

Almustafa loved his people and yearned for them in their mountain hamlets, coveted by eagles but clawed by an alien tyranny and a tyranny within.

But it was here in Orphalese, the city of his exile, that he, with the rage for Life in him, had blazed with his loftiest songs – and received his worthiest tributes.

In the city's bustling streets and thoughtful assemblies and on the rims of the vast plains and lakes that stretched out beyond it, he had attained visions of a wisdom he had sought with the desperation of a drowning man and the confidence of a prophet. Among the city's people he discovered a new family in whose liberal hearts he set his restive roots and preened his winged words.

And the people loved him, for he voiced to them their own silent yearning for their greater selves which often lay unfulfilled in their more mundane pursuits. And it was that restlessness in them which blended with his own and went on to inform the Book he had brought forth amongst them, its very words fringing the traffic of their days and fanning the embers of their dreams.

But now he was dying. It may have been that his body had drunk so much of the contradictions of the world as it struggled to meld them into harmony that it became worn out by its own exertions. Or it may have been that his mission was to be crowned by some wondrous act or speech as he stood in death's doorway.

Would death allow him the dignity of a parting communion or the solace of a hidden welcome? Or should he be content with the fleeting warmth of Life, whose bosom he was loath to leave?

The people of Orphalese had heard of his illness, and a delegation came to plead with him to shun the ghostly hand that was upon him, and to ask of his wisdom. Little did they know that they were to take part in a rite of great power and mystery which would attend his journey and hint at what lay beyond it.

An elder of the city drew near to him as he stood on a hillock looking out towards the sea; and he said, Sweet Reed of God and breath of his vast being, we are troubled to hear of your pain. Long have you been Healer and Helmsman of our souls. Would that you could submit your woe to our doctors so that we might be spared a greater woe?

And Almustafa turned to look upon the people, and his heart went out to them in love and sympathy.

In their old and young faces, he saw, as in a large sweeping mirror, fragments of his own past life, even of his numinous life to come. For in them and in their children and grand-children he might yet travel as a memory and an urge.

But his eyes, roaming over the human countenance of his adopted city, sought after Almitra, who was not among the crowd.

The Seeress had been his first convert, and, for some score years in Orphalese, his soul mate and the gentle but bold hand that grasped the feral flames of his words and tuned them to the speech of that city.

And though she had, on one occasion, unlaced the orchard of her body to a passing sorrow of his, he did not reach for the fruit; for, he, whose mission was to conquer all fear, feared that his anguish of a day might taint her generosity for the days to come. And when, on that day, she conferred on his lips a favour, he savoured it as a searing testimony to a larger presence and a confirmation of a calling long etched in his chest. So, the twain sailed on, their mainsails billowing in the same wind but not entangled in the howling storm nor mangled on the raw reef.

Of late, though, the Seeress had found the domestic harbour her soul had long spurned even as it yearned for it in her silent seafaring.

And Almustafa blessed Almitra's happiness in her new-found wharf, but he ached for her, as no other living mortal could administer as *she* had done to the restlessness of his mind or soothe the wilder passions of his soul and offer them a haven.

Still, with a heart loosened from his pain and from the spectre's chill and rippling with the brilliance of a dying star, he said:

I thank you my friends for your loving kindness. The years I have spent among you are but a cluster in the infinite meadows of time. And yet in their passionate midst I have grown to embrace many a joy and burn with more than one glimpse of eternity.

An individual life is brief, but as she courses through the veins of the larger Life, she partakes of the timeless pulse of the greater passion and of its hidden purpose.

Truly, she is but a heartbeat of that wider yearning, her own veins having been forged in Life's own fierce expansion and self-wonder.

And as she presses on with her journey, she will come to know much joy as she sheds one garment and dons another, even as she glides in blessèd nakedness.

And I have known much pleasure, and much good pain, as my sapling soul stretched out, ravenous, to meet the sun.

But it was your belief in me, vague as I was then, vague as I am now, that has guided my sightless roots and urged my infant stalk into the light.

The healing you say I have wrought was but a laying-on of your hands on my soul, which, as it rose in gratitude to hail its patron, broke into the sweat of the myrtle and was sweetly received by the gracious air.

And, though I bless all your doctors and healers, I would have you know, be it to lighten your hearts, that I am not a wilting iris, but a thistledown quivering on the brink of a vast journey; not a fading cinder, but a spark raring to seek the greater Fire.

Then an officer said, Why would you leave our city, secure and resplendent in her towering walls and sunny youths, to journey, as we fear you might, into the kingdom of silence and desolation? Would you but tarry a while longer for us to see you walking on our lanes with silver in your hair and gold on your lips?

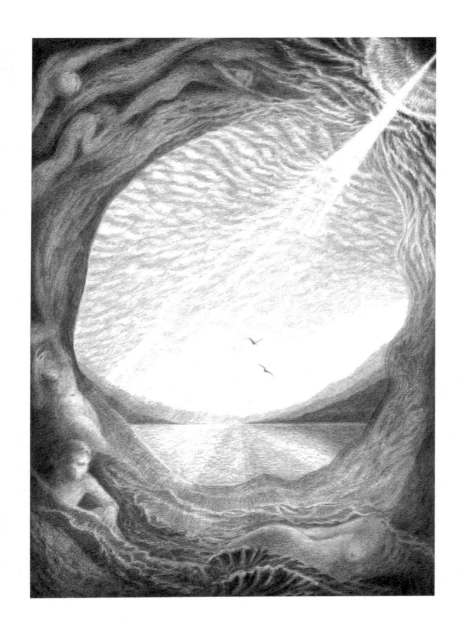

15

And Almustafa in answering him began to say:

No quibbler am I with Life or with the children of Life, being one of them.

Nor have I been shy to drink from her wellsprings and cups, even from her puddles when my lips were parched; for they who spurn her gifts commit a wrong against her and against themselves and the Most High, who is also the Most Near.

Others may have lectured to you about denial and the sovereignty of the ascetic life.

But I have at no time praised the chastening of the body to woo the soul.

And yet, since we are all fragments, nay the very living cells, of a greater Body, we must move with the laws that govern the births and deaths of chrysanthemums and stars.

Death may be no more than a name, and yet it can be the impulse that lifts us from our slough, and the condiment that transforms our bland supper into a feast.

We are haunted by the idea of death, and yet that idea can be an eagle that may pluck us from our timid backyards and lift us to the daring summits, where we may find a greater eagle to take us beyond the clouds.

It is death, so named, that has inspired us to build our greatest shrines and sing our most enduring songs. Aye, and to shed our dearest tears!

Verily, death is a grand teacher of Life; and we would cling to every face and each song on our path if we were to know we would die the next day. The lightest brush of our lips against the death-cup would send us back to Life parching for every dewdrop on the shivering leaf. Blue as sapphire would seem the sky and as a dimple in a babe's cheek the frantic highway. The humblest cottage in the distance would be draped in mystery and the world in a splendour unseen before.

Aye, death is the shadow that illumines our essence. But since the touch of a floating thread in the dark can enmesh the mind of a man in a net of fear, I too needs examine the spaces and the cobwebs in my own mind and find out if my life is fit to be garlanded by death – whether I can *blossom* into silence. I too needs look at my life-record to see if I can journey beyond it with few tears over unheeded windows and unshared moments. For a record burdened with these may not be brought to the Altar or to the glow of the Holy Fire. And it may well be that what we fear most is not death itself but the *incompleteness* of Life.

But blessed is the yearning of this city for her peacefulness and triumph over terror, and for her wholeness, even as she stokes the roar of her foundries; for from them there shall rise bridges that will cast off their steel to soar as gentler and astral visions. And I may then be a spirit feather in that great flight, aye even as a wave sighing after the full moon.

And a young soldier came forward, and said, What say you, then, of our heroes, those who die in battle so that we may live and prosper? Will you bless them too?

And he, lapped in peace, answered:

In blessing all the children of Life, I but enunciate with the lips of the Mother and shiver in her many-coloured plumage. For, She will dote on the slow and the silent, even as they bend down to weave their cocoons or plait their coral; aye, even as the days file by them with fanfare or beat upon their tenderness with rude curiosity. And She will pity the weak and the diffident, even as they cower into a nook or tilt their wings in fright before the hurtling hawk.

But She will also bless those who surge and

sparkle with mighty longing and resolve. For to sit still is to ape the stagnant pool – though there too Life coils in myriad forms, pining to join the zephyr-footed, crystal-breasted stream.

No, I would have none slight the hero amongst you.

As he rises to his destiny you rise with him kindled and expanded by his fiery surge, even as the tail of a comet follows its flaming core into the vast zodiac. And he intoxicates you as he pours out the red wine of his youth on the desolate sand, mocking the old age that will not lay a cold finger on him. And he exalts you even as he humbles you; yeah as he towers above the game of chance and as he flings his wager to the bloated war dragon in the rumble of drums and under the numbness of the stars.

Sword in hand, he charges, not so much his fellow struggler across the field, but War itself and all its engines, raucous and futile, hoping in his unfathomed mind to fell its vulture-machinery and stem the lust for it in the minds of men – aye, even as he takes their breath away with the terrible beauty of his charge!

No, I would have none slight the hero – or the heroine. But I would ask you to see in their

calm gaze man's fear embraced for an instant by a brave dream!

And yet I would ask you to spare a thought for the coward. For in his dithering and quaking there too is a glimpse of Life, in her cunning limberness.

And in his dumping of the sword there is courage, and a subtle empathy with Life that keens for her martyred children and would not be consoled, having been so rudely overruled.

And there is courage in his desertion and in his embracing of shame, for many a sung hero has rushed into the fray spurred more by the officer's bark behind him than the plea of the frayed banner in the wind.

And the two, the hero and the coward, shall reside together in heaven, which is this very world in its greater expansion, and shall see the wisdom of their acts.

And the foes of the past, those who had known each other as vague columns in the mist or as mangled grins among the crushed heather, shall sit together and bless their scars into lutes and sing of the pity and uselessness of War.

And a woman, ablaze with loveliness, raised a dulcet but taunting voice and said

to him, But, in the harsh meantime, what of the death that destroys our youth and robs us of the warmth and softness of our bodies in barter for the cold and foul grave?

And Almustafa looked upon the woman, and roseate petals swayed like drunken sailors in his great hazel eyes even as dark eddies assailed them with grim sobriety; and he said:

Too proud are we to yield our bodies, pampered and clothed by our fear, to the earth.

But is not the earth the very crucible of our frames? Was not our firmness and our suppleness formed in the core of her vessel and on her great potter's wheel?

Would we not return a borrowed tool by the lender claimed? Even with gratitude for the time gained in its custody?

And an old woman interrupted him with her own undefeated fire, saying, Truly, when I was young, I took delight in gazing upon my face in the mirror and in studying the smoothness of my cheek and the ripeness of my lips. I rejoiced at the thrust of my bosom, the slenderness of my waist and the lissome stretch of my figure. These I nourished with rare fruits and prized potions. And the men groaned even to touch my arm and shivered like leaves in the wind as they lay at my breast. Yeah, the lover with the eye scornful of the world would fret and grovel on his knees like a parched dog panting for the rose's dew. But, as the years wore on I watched the invisible ploughs stealthily, stubbornly, etching their furrows into my forehead, and I listened to the soundless wings of the crows that came at night and left their feet-marks by the corners of my eyes. And now I am in the people's parlance a hag and in my mirror an abomination, even as the obstinate dew on the withered rose dreams of the lover waylaid by the murderous road!

And Almustafa inclined with great gentleness towards the old woman. In her countenance he saw the courage and grief of a dearly beloved face and the radiant and righteous rage of his previous inquisitor and of all women.

But as he was about to respond to her, a mist rose into his eyes and his right hand came up to study the mist. The people thought this was a sign for them to depart, but he steadied them with his left hand, even as the mist swarmed beneath his fingers and radiated through his veins.

And he shivered as a cold hyacinth-scented breeze ruffled his garment and tingled his skin. But the mist took him into its heart, and he felt strangely warmed.

And he journeyed into the mist.

And from within it there arose, like a surging dawn, the face of a woman.

And the woman gazed upon him with exceeding tenderness and pity; and she bent down as though to clasp him to her bosom.

And he looked up, dazed and adrift, into the woman's heavy-lidded hazel eyes. And in them he saw a sea of sadness that belonged to a former life brightening under a breaking joy.

And though bewildered and unsure, he became as one with the woman's eyes.

Through them he saw a ship sailing on a turquoise sea into a scarlet sunset. On the stern stood a man holding a handkerchief, which he did not wave about but would in time cover his face, mosquito-chewed, in the mushy soil of a primeval forest. And he saw the contorted face of an infant at the woman's arm, wailing and twisting above the tide-chiselled shingle of the shore.

And he was assailed by a great loneliness welling up inside his host. And he felt the enormous weight of a white-crusted mountain whose rugged side the woman was beginning to ascend while an abyss tugged at the corners of her eyes. Then he saw an altar cracked in the front like an ancient cup and the face of another man, imperious and desperate.

And on the periphery of a cluster of stone houses with red-tiled roofs he saw a house similarly fashioned but set apart, a slightly crooked pine tree inclining over its low roof. And inside the house he was led to a narrow bed a-squat by the wall of a frugal room. And he experienced a cascade of spasms and a medley of other tremors culminating in a great convulsion, and he was thrust into an immensity of glare and coldness and noise.

He was now able to see with his own eyes and feel with his own sentient skin.

And he began to hear, even sense, the landing of snowflakes on the craggy terraces and the bursting open of pine cones on their branches and the flutter of the lobes of wild dill. And he was at one with the village symphony of lullabies and prayers and pro-fanities, punctuated by moans of stolen pleasures in licit and forbidden beds from inside the red-roofed houses. A while later he was in the middle of a vault set into the mountainside. Haunting litanies echoed along the roughly hewn walls encircling him. He then drifted through a maze of stony corridors and out into a jewelled night. But as he lifted up his face heavenwards, his eyes were filled with the flickering of innumerable lamps streaming away in the vast blackness towards a huge light-framed door. And on the strange, ineffable wood of the door he saw his own fists, a child's, hammering, hammering, hammering!

Then, nearer at hand and in daylight, he saw a great cedar tree on the furrowed snow-mantled slope of the mountain. And he saw a man stepping out of its massive lizard-skin trunk.

The man was holding a glittering orb in his left hand; and he was smiling benignly as he came towards him carrying a sharpened pen in his right hand.

And the image of the man metamorphosed into that of a winged being, an angel. And the angel, clasping the pen, advanced towards him with a cryptic look in his astral eyes.

And the wings of the angel arched upwards and spread out across the sky as he bent over him. And the angel etched something into his chest with the sharp tip of the pen, which he felt resonating in his body. Then the angel drew his great face nearer to him and touched his lips with his own. They seared his slight mouth, overwhelming it and the core of his being with the fire of stars and the yoke of a gift and a mission. And he felt as if he now knew, as a skylark or a dolphin might know, the mind of Life, and he was filled with her fearlessness and her love

and pity and promise for all her feuding children. The face then withdrew and the wings wilted, their lowest feathers brushing against his chest, gathering unto their snowy satin a few stains of brilliant blood. Then they flickered and paled along with the angelic form only to resurge as two giant pine trees towering over the assortment of tile-roofed houses, brooding grottoes, and plumbless ravines.

But before the angel's beautifully forlorn face faded completely, one of his eyes melted into cascading crystal and then congealed into the contour of a cave set against the mountainside.

And he walked into the dank darkness of the cave, and stood on the lip of a gurgling well-spring, and he felt the tug of the great sea.

But another heaving power, that of the people of Orphalese, drew him back into their anxious midst. The earlier vision had endured but a moment and the mist stayed its hand. So, braced by the vision of his homeland and confirmed in his power over the Stalker, Almustafa found his words and said to the old woman:

Brave is the eye journeying into the mirror's bustling solitude! And blessed is the rose with its tenacious dew!

But let not the looking glass or the hurtling traveller be the judge of your beauty.

From *within* shall beauty shine forth, like a fountain of endless yearnings and infinite mysteries.

Beauty has the whole world as a playground, even as a fane, and will not be gauged by the tailor's measure or the merchant's scales.

And like beauty, youth is not defined by the almanac or ruled by the weathervane. It is a cornucopia, a delirium, of blossoms, heedless unto the seasons, a restless urge, be it within an ancient olive tree busy fulfilling her role, wherein lies the beauty of one's existence. And a role will not be judged by the height of its leap or the wideness of its arm-span, for in the goldfinch's nest and the toy maker's spinning top there is enough enchantment to make a *world* whirl in wonder and merriment. Nor will it be appraised by the loudness it tosses in the air, for in the seamstress's pondering and the crab's hermitage there is a silver silence that spurs to rapture the strings of the cosmic lute.

And the people were emboldened by Almustafa's resurgence. And another woman who held a babe to her bosom, said, But what of our children, O man of charmed words? Surely a mother would not surrender her child to Death! She, who was heavy

with the growing mystery of him as the moon toyed with the waves month after month after month, can do naught but shield her child from the Claw, aye, shield him even with the shivering walls of her heart! How can she but live her days and nights in fear of the Shadow falling upon the playpen of the toddler and the path of the youth! Surely, Death is an axe that would cut off our yearlings from our embraces, from what they might be! How can a mother speak to her child of Death save as the foremost Enemy? How can she ever find solace or meaning or fellowship in life if her babe is ripped away from her? Indeed, the very heavens would then tumble, a dumb monstrosity, into her soul, and the shards of God's lanterns would glow like infernal embers in the ashes of her heart! God himself would seem to be an unnatural father, a savage and cruel tyrant who enjoys bestowing a favour on his peons only to snatch it away from them as they kneel to do him homage!

And he, swaying like a cypress in the wind, said:

Praise be to the mystery of motherhood that holds the rapt threads of the world! Aye, even as the father, not seen at the table, sheds a tear for the fish gasping in his net!

A babe is born into our riddle unlettered in the fear of death. But those who have children will see in them an extension of their own breath and they will treasure them and be fearful for them. And yet who would want a babe to remain in the cradle all his life or be swaddled for evermore in his elders' fears?

Like a cedar you may wish your child to be. But what is a cedar without her hardy soil and exalted air, the shimmering of the heavens in her bristly leaves, the traffic of memories in her sap, and her Lebanon?

Teach your child, or better still, allow him to learn, the steps and sweeps of the great dance in which all take part and are at one, moving with daring and compassion and skill.

And when you visit the graves of your fore-bears with your child invite him to pray for those who have been weaned from their bodies. For a child's prayer finds its way unhindered to God's ear.

And a child's prayer for the dead is an education for the child, a softening and a strengthening, even as the heritage of those he prays for is clamouring in his bone-marrow.

The sorrow, the vast sorrow, is for those who fail to grasp the essence of their being even as it lies within reach of their understanding. Pity the songs, the dawn choruses, orphaned on the abandoned branch!

And as your child needs to rejoice in the music so needs he to savour the silence. For in it there is a speechless hymn for times past and times yet in the womb. And what is silence but the gasp of the string before it shivers into melody and rejoins the immeasurable choir? And what is silence but the beginning of wisdom? And might it not be its very summit?

All is his birthright. And though he would journey through life as a pilgrim rather than a conqueror, he would know that Life's gifts are his by inheritance to share with Life's other children in love and graciousness.

Pity the child who sees the tide washing away his sandcastle and forgets that tide when he becomes a man.

And pity those who will not soar with the thought that a lantern nourished by the holy oil can be diminished only in the embrace of the greater light and that its dimness will be as a moment's idling of the albatross before he rises to his destiny unencumbered.

And an old man, a retired tax collector, shuffled forward receiving grim looks from the people around him; and he said, Disease has come upon me like a swarm of locusts, gnawing my body to the bone, stripping it of all but despair and anger. I shall welcome Death if he deigns to take my agonies and ravings away. And yet, should I not cleave to some hope that I might be rendered hale once more?

And Almustafa said:

Even the seraphs who are fashioned of *absolute* joy will melt *absolutely* in the full beauty of God's face.

Equally, a man's heart may *burst* with too much happiness. Aye or it might collapse into a hard and incurious lump.

Pain, being a twin and a partner to joy, may pace itself to give a piquant charm to the glad moments.

But pain perpetual is a bale unbearable, even for a seraph; and *he* can lift an Alp with a feather of his wing! Have you not heard of *him* who could not endure the pain of seeing God loving a new creation?

Verily, man will *not* be a slave to pain, save to the winged wound of love. But even when pain seems to have turned the air to stone and barred all light, Hope will stretch *her* wings in the confined space and the vault will split asunder.

So invoke Hope to your aid, and she will come, for she is more enduring than pain and more resolute.

And when pain is clasping you to its prickly chest in the wheezing room, *she* is flying under the stars soliciting prayers and angels and healers to come to your aid.

Have you not heard of the poet who drank poison in rage at his indifferent town, only to hear, as his last breath loitered in his throat, a knock on the door — the prince of the land coming to celebrate the unacknowledged genius?

Behold the slender fox pursued by the hounds and the slight ant tantalised by the puckish boy! See their unquestioning flight on to the viaducts and straws of Life, their wild clinging to her ropes and ruses!

But strive, my friend, to cultivate calm and re-build, even out of your pain, and the doubts that may shadow it, the ever-ready bridge to Life. For if the final ceremony is graced by calm then it is an offering fit to place on the holy table.

We are born with the urge to live, not to die.

And yet how can the flute sing if not severed from the tree and pierced by the knife? And if not broken by the sun and borne away by the wind, can the brine of the sea nourish the orchard? And without the sting of the flame how can the incense glow with fondness and dissolve in perfume?

And whose woe is greater than the woe of God, whose joy is greater than all joy?

Then a lean man, a dispenser of drugs, said, Would you tell us of medicine?

And he answered saying:

Time and again we go out into the fields looking for herbs that would bring us healing. But often the roots of our restoration are lodged deep within us.

And though the flowers of the lea and those that cling to the wind-swept cliffs would unravel their ancient memories to us, we would need to partake of their darker visions also.

They had baked under the sun and shivered in the icy nights when we were but a thought in God's mind.

In truth, they had been stirring in the dark red earth long before she felt the footfall of man or the keenness of his plough or indeed the fever of his brow laid to rest in her deep coolness.

Through their veins the shudders of the young earth ran and gave birth to the oracular flesh of their fruits prophesying other flesh and other harvests.

And in them coursed in equal measures the bitterness and sweetness of creation.

Is not the healing power of the ill-flavoured leaf a parable that never fades in the telling?

Truly, there is no malady without a medicine. For they too come in pairs. But the cure may lie, if not within the sufferer, then upon the lips of a nameless flower in a remote wilderness or in an idea that will one day visit the mind of a woman or a man not yet born.

And though man, in the panic of his days, has often sought to separate his pains and medicines, he will in the ripeness of time learn the wholeness of healing.

But he will have to learn first the wholeness of pain.

And he will know that as his body elements need to work in harmony with one another, so does his body need to act in concert with the body of all mankind.

Behold the mother who went out into the

forest to seek a healing plant for a dying neighbour only to discover a cure for her own ailing child.

And consider the man who robbed another of a rare elixir but drank it as an affliction and a poison.

And even though men will travel long distances and pay in gold for subtle cures, a simple balm, like a loving touch or a word of forgiveness, can travel equally far, and nearer home.

The day will surely come when a hundred years will be a mere phase in a man's life.

And yet the lengthening of your days will not placate your fear of parting. Rather, it will fan it to a frenzy, since what is to be lost will seem even dearer in your eyes. And science itself which would have made this possible would turn into a cold priesthood dispensing its wares to the rich and the powerful who in time would use science as their tool and lackey.

Immortality is a peak which is ever mocking the ropes that try to scale it; for it is ever disappearing into the brilliance of God's laughter. And science will always try to deny death its dominion and finality, thus exercising the divinity within us which looks at such ultimatums as an illusion. But the scientist knows in his heart of hearts that the young sapling in the shade of the oak tree must have a share in the light and that the forest must always renew itself.

Strive, rather, for the *quality* of your life instead of its length and for its fellowships instead of its conquests. For a brief life, and Life is never brief, that has merit in it is better than a long one without benefit to one's soul or to others. And a man carrying the weight but not the wisdom of years will plead to be delivered of his freight.

Blessed be the day when medicine will be for awareness and for wholeness and when it will not be sought for power nor sold for profit, replacing one affliction with another.

And blessed be the greater day when no medicine will be sold or bought, because it will not be needed.

And even though you will scour the earth and the minds of women and men of all times for a cure and will crown with laurel the temples of healers, know you well that when the doctor drops her hands in resignation, a prayer may reach the source of all healing.

Can you not hear in every human supplication the whisper of God spurring the prayer?

Strive, therefore, for total healing; for healing is like the coming of Spring. The call of the red-winged blackbird under the grey clouds is surely a glad omen. But it is when the columbines and the buttercups and the rose mallows fill the bed of the forest and the jay and the bluebird and the purple martin its canopy that we say Spring has truly come.

And an old scholar said, What if Death robs me of the chance to finish my book, on which I have been toiling for many years?

And Almustafa saw – as in a passing vision – the orphanage of his own words but also their many parents and numerous offspring.

And the vision took possession of him. And it carried his thoughts to the sea of his earlier trance which he was now seeing from the bow of a large ship ploughing the waves. And he saw more children, two doe-eyed girls and an older generous-faced boy, by his side on the ship's bow.

And as he looked into the distant horizon he saw the headstone of the first boy and that of the younger of the two girls. And the hazel eyes of the woman who was also on the ship melted and were slowly reshaping themselves into a third headstone.

But before the woman's eyes had so changed, they seemed to invite him into their implacable sadness but undaunted yearning. And as he leaned towards them in sombre submission, they fluttered like a falcon un-hooded, a fire in them flaming out like a dancer with wings, swaying and twirling, a happy sprite. They led him past a colossal woman of copper and into a strange city. And he saw curious carriages and bustling bazaars and gaudily decorated booths, where crystal orbs conducted him into rooms full of images and tomes floating in the air and twisting like drunken auroras.

Then a lanky knight in armour trotted up on a tall auburn horse whose eyes blazed like sun-mated wine. And the knight beckoned to him as he stood, small and forsaken, in a dim narrow lane. And the knight stretched forth his arm, lapped in chainmail, to hoist his little frame on to the high saddle behind him.

And they rode into a forest of white poplar trees with large argent leaves growing on their branches. And one of the leaves detached itself from the branch of a gigantic tree in their path and as it grew larger and larger it shaped itself into a boat. And the boat, having invited him from the saddle into its hold, took him across the same great sea he had sailed on before, this time facing incessant dawns.

Then the leaf-boat rustled against the shingle of a turquoise-lipped shore and shuddered, changing into *an eagle. And the eagle lifted him to the summit of the white mountain of his earlier vision.*

And nestling under the snow-capped summit was the village of the small stone houses with red-tiled roofs.

And beneath a walnut tree just outside the village there sat the man with the imperious and desperate look. And there was a flicker of pity in the pride-hewn face of the man, but he turned away seeming as truculent as ever, though a tentative tear half-gleamed in his left eye.

And Almustafa invoked the tear to rise and respire between his own eyelids. And through its liberating crystal he saw and understood a little more.

He saw the misery of the tax collector and the grief of the hangman. He drifted into the nightmares of the pasha and the doubts of the patriarch, and he shook with the fear of the guard and the sobbing of the harlot. He was moved by great compassion for them all, even for the priests of feuding faiths who were glowering at his yet unborn words and declaring him an impostor and a heretic; even for the kadis who were decreeing his death and the mobs, who, rouser-driven, were coiling and writhing in the streets like a fabulous beast spewing obscenities. But as he was assailed again and again by the sight of the arrogant, ermine-robed emir sitting in judgement over the

obeisant peasants, he vowed to speak to them of the
rage of the great sea and the dignity of the bald eagle.
All the while, he could feel his youthful fingernails
clawing at the sky, clawing, clawing, clawing.

All this came to pass in Almustafa's mind as
he stood and swayed on his feet for an instant in
front of the people, whose attraction again drew
him back into their eager presence. Retrieving
his thoughts, he answered the old scholar saying:

Each will write their book. The books *will*
be written, if not by their authors, then by
their authors' children, or grandchildren, or a
mere passer-by catching a word in the wind
and weaving from it a tale on his or her own
loom.

Words may indeed seem feeble and brittle,
readily bruised in the jostle of memories and
easily charred by the rabid torch. But, frail as
they seem to be, they have a strength that
mocks the flame and a permanence that baffles
the censor's sponge. And they will find their
own path to the blessed Garden.

The face which a painter loosens from the
rainbow or a poet from his imaginings may be
as real as Life and as durable. And like her it
offers its lineaments to untold readings and its
longing to countless wings.

The book *will* be written, even by the unlettered, and in the alphabets of speech and deed and dream. And each will hold their book proudly but also humbly as they stand before the Reader of all words and acts and silences.

Some will write for glory, and they shall be rewarded with the garlands of victors. And some will write for riches, and they shall be paid with the treasure of inner contentment. And some will write to elude pain and loneliness, and they shall be bathed in the river of healing and fellowship. And some will write for the love of truth or Man or God, and they shall be clothed in the breezy garments of saints.

And know you well that the words which you have plucked from the green lexicon shall exude the sweet yearning and the mighty resolve of all the children of Life who had gathered them before you and placed them as *you* would – as an offering under the great Tree.

Hallowed is that gift! And what a priest might judge to be sullied and lowly, the Great Soul might bless and exalt above all the stately litanies sung to her in the gilded temple.

Be calm in the knowledge that even your very thoughts will not be lost; and though some of them may not find their way to parchment or stone, they will survive and inhabit spaces and beings unknown to you, even as you may stand on the shore but cannot see the ship sailing beyond the sea line.

But you need to let go of your book and allow it to travel unfettered by your pain or pride.

Like the spirit, a book will not be shackled to one body. What warbler would sing from the same branch every day and night of the Spring?

And what joy greater to a singer than to hear her song issuing from other throats and other dreams?

Truly, all who live are leaves in the great Book which is ever mindful of its green children scattered within its unbounded heart.

And an old sailor, one who had dropped anchor in many a harbour and bore many a merry scar, surged forward and asked, And what of Time and change?

And a smile rose like a spirited wave onto the face of Almustafa; and remembering the seas he had crossed and the harbours he sojourned in and the ecstasies and scars he had won while the anchor of his ship dosed in the dark water, he answered saying:

Time is the vast sea which Man will sail upon. But between the hoisting of the canvas and the folding of it Man is transformed by every wave the keel of his boat cleaves into liquid laughter.

And Man is so taken up with his dream of an island where the leaves of the trees never turn yellow that he fails to grasp that the waves of the sea are but a heaving of his own breast. And only in learning to sail through change can he find the peaceful isle, and only in bidding the crests and tumbles of his journey to echo within his being and be restored to harmony therein can he claim to have known the ways of the sea or savoured the joys of seafarers.

Then he can be a wave of the ocean even as he sits in the shade of the palm tree.

Readily will I tell you, Time is not a thread unrolling neatly from one shore to another.

Protean as it is, one of its mintage is mercury!

But many are those who fear to be left out of Time's logbook or be marooned behind its flighty leaves. So they surround themselves with clocks and calendars. But these will not truly tell the time. They cannot even tell a man's age – never mind a woman's!

But the cities of men have made themselves slaves to the false records and would not recognise the innermost recorder.

They have set up a cult and a roaring trade out of the unlined face, and would not find it profitable to acknowledge the mannerless bloom within.

Would that we had clocks and almanacs that told of our soul's striving and of the fortunes of our winged thoughts and plodding vows!

So let us read in the lines etched in the forehead a rich record and a plucky testimony.

It is a busy brow and a calloused palm that may speak more eloquently of the traffic in compassion and of the glow of wisdom's granary.

The artist who tries to please his patron by painting a face free of the lettering of years is being uncivil to his benefactor.

For, to grow is a sign that we are in concert with Nature, garnering freely from her open basket.

And a portrait that blots out the unruly marks is unmaking the beauty of individual life.

And a ship stranded in the lush cove will see her sails rotting in the indolent air and her hull encumbered by barnacles.

It is when she is sweeping under a billowy sail that she is least brooding on the constrictor-weeds.

But there is wisdom also in brooding; for it is from the Winter's fond pondering that the Spring inherits its blossoms and perfumes.

And in the dark cellar will the juice of the vine shed its sour memories as it makes ready for the king's feast.

Truly, change is the terrible passion of the grape as it turns into celestial wine, lifted by death, patient and proud, but touched only by God's lips.

And a judge asked, What in your ruling will happen on the fabled Day of Summoning, and will there be a Last Judgement?

And he, ever loath to passing judgement or to being judged, least of all by his own musings, answered saying:

You shall be gathered into the mind of God from which you were sent forth.

And the trumpet that shall recall you sounds even now — even through your heartbeats and the breeze that ruffles your raiment.

The aeons of time are as a twinkling of the universal Eye. And the grave shall gape in awe and surrender its charge.

But the summoning shall be a homecoming, and it shall be marked by celebration rather than chastisement, and by understanding instead of torment.

Yet the understanding shall be so over-powering that there will be pain with the bursting of ignorance as with the shedding of injustice, for the inequities of the world of men have long cried out for redress.

But through the pain there will come joy. And from the bitterness of some of the seeds we sowed in ignorance there shall blossom a sweet healing.

Would that there was fairness in the world dispensed by human laws! But since it is not so, the hope for perfection beyond the coffin timber will endure, even as this hope may allow the rich to get richer and the poor poorer, the oppressor more impudent and the oppressed more timid and forlorn.

Like the certainty of Spring is the home-coming and as opulent as the dew!

There is a homecoming even while the shop-keeper is counting his silver and the young mother is easing her babe against her breast and the constable winds his way through the night streets.

Homecoming is a daily traffic between earth and heaven and between one soul and another. Rather than being an affair wedded to the end of time, it is a state that is already coming to pass, and is putting forth new shoots and beginnings even as we stand here and send our thoughts to and fro.

Aye, the day of reckoning can stretch to an aeon or compress into an instant. And the dark will be anointed by the light, because it was a twin to it and a fellow wayfarer.

And you will be asked what you have done with your life and what offerings you have made.

And the humblest of gifts will be accepted and blessed. Have you not heard of the desert dweller who brought a skin of brackish water to the king's palace, deeming it a rare gift? And the wise king was pleased with the favour and praised the nomad's discernment!

And that day will be a day of learning and triumph.

For whosoever truly believes and cleaves unto Life shall be in fellowship with her, forever sustained, the very moment in whose breadth he made his pledge to her forever betrothed to eternity.

Nor would his labours be allowed to crumble into naught.

For even when we trespass against Life in an instant of thoughtlessness or pique, Life will allow us, once we have regained our harmony, to reclaim our heritage.

And we shall sit down by the River of Infinite Tales and by the Ocean of All Possibilities and we shall converse with the scattered lovers and petals returning to the great Garden and the mariners and pearls shedding their hulls and hermitages at the great Harbour.

Yeah, on that day, which even now is coming to pass, the snow will melt and the daisies and the primroses and the sweet violets will venture into the daylight.

And on that day we shall know each other and draw all the laughing veils of God.

And when the loving radiance fills everything, where can Hades be?

Then a jeweller asked, What of Enlightenment, and how can we journey into its brilliance?

And he said:

In the course of time, we shall come to the light of all things. But we may need to trek long in the passionate darkness; for Enlightenment, like a proud queen, will not bestow her favours upon a sluggard.

But in the bustle of their days, men expect to attain Enlightenment even as they unwrap the bundle they have bought in the marketplace.

And who could say they might not?

But as a seed of wheat will need time – and grace – to rise to its destiny, so will the germ of your awareness begin to grow when cradled by the greater Providence.

It may well be that a sudden downpour may jolt a sleeping mind into an awakening even as the bean caper shudders into leaf with the coming of rain, Yeah, be it after years of mortal drought.

For *there* also the yearning for bloom would have been simmering long in the lean pouch like a hermit in his retreat.

Behold the traveller who roamed for Enlightenment in faraway places, but would have met with her in his own backyard.

And consider the scholar who sought her in the heaping of facts, but would have attained a vision of her in one or more home truths had he not deemed them slight and unbecoming.

And yet Enlightenment is not a tame pet curled up by the fire, though she may assume such a guise. Often she is a hunter and a pilgrim forever hurtling past her quarry and beyond her shrine.

And she is a flight of freedom that will pluck you from the shaded grooves of your habits and peel away the widowhood of your eyes to wed them to the wonders of heaven and earth.

Enlightenment unfolds wholly when your mind merges with a greater mind even as the river pours into the sea and becomes one with it and as the lovers fade to grow in each other's delight.

Then you will rise from the narrowness of grasping into the expansiveness of the open and generous palm which spans the universe.

But you will need to present your Enlightenment to the whole of Life, of whom you are part.

And you will present her with humility but also with the certitude of a barn owl in the silence of her pinions and the keenness of her talons.

And all those with whom you have made peace, be it in thought, will come to attend upon you and grant you more strength and rejoicing.

And all those you have blessed in mid-flight,

approving of their freedom, be it from your own love, will come and bless you and tender more happy horizons under your flight feathers.

You have seen the conjurer bring forth a bird from the 'empty' air. But *you* are the true enchanter, and you shall unlock from within your space the casements quivering unheeded at the periphery of your mind.

When you partake of the wisdom of the universe, you become a sharer in its fearlessness. And when you hear the Door whining on its hinges in the night you will be prepared, even with a smile on your face, though a *saint* may be visited by an instant of doubt.

And you will be seized by the ecstasy of Enlightenment, even as a child is seized by the largess of the festive day. But you will learn that this is but your inheritance coming back to claim you.

In truth, it will be a happy remembering, even as the salamander pokes his benumbed nose from beneath his winter log and gazes at the sun-dappled woodland.

And you will whirl in dance and weep for your ignorance, but you will also laugh at it in good humour as though it were the antics of a dearly beloved child.

And yet you will not boast of your Enlightenment. Rather, you will be like a babe restored to its mother's breast.

And as your body will be bathed in water, so will your soul be bathed in light.

And when your soul is so bathed, it will be immersed in a sea that is *beyond* good and evil and beyond division. And it will dissolve in a sky that knows *no* height or depth, *nor* prayer or answer.

The path to Enlightenment may start with wonder and may be paved by pain, but it must be attended by love and compassion. It is a dark and desolate house that is full of gilded chairs but will not admit the scruffy angel asking for alms at the door.

Truly, the light will fill you wholly when you can relate to the ant-lion in its pit as to the nun in her cloister, and when you can see in the hawk eyes of the moth's wings the same holy force that braided the sinews of the great whale.

And where an ordinary man sees darkness and emptiness, an enlightened one sees light and seraphs in conversation with humans and daffodils.

And when an ordinary man sees suffering

and he curses it, an enlightened person sees an ocean of pearls streaming back to God's tearful face. And he would journey from one cosmos to another, though filling them all; and he would travel as a pilgrim to the holy place, but once there, the sanctuary would lift up the song and humble itself before him.

Yes, Enlightenment is as the exalted queen who will spurn a measly suitor; but she is also the sovereign who will not rest until she has clasped the fierce lover to her most radiant bosom.

Would not an instant in that embrace be worthier than an aeon under the cosy snuffer?

And a young scholar enquired, Do we need a mentor to see us through our paces in this world and across to what may loiter or sprawl beyond it?

And he, kneeling in thought to many a soaring memory, answered saying:

It is a hallowed joy to sit at the feet of a teacher and cleave, like a jasmine branch, unto the gate of his wisdom. But were that gate to be as tall as a cypress or a king's tower you would have to find your own height and unfetter your own fragrance.

Your teacher may clothe you in his very

mantle. And it will warm you when the hedgehog is curled beneath the frozen leaves, and it will give you coolness when the bumble-bee is flitting drowsily amongst the golden thistles.

But in time you will need to weave your own cloth and cut your own raiment, for in it you will feel the pulse of your own labour and the wing-beats of your own yearnings, and you will be reminded and vindicated by them through the seasons – before you cast that same garment to the laughing wind.

He, who has caught the song of heaven and baffled the prison walls, will spur you into the heart of joy, helping you toss away the scriptures and laws that impede your dance to rapture.

And he will baptise you into Life, who will draw you further into her mighty embrace and fill you with her endurance and transform you with her mystery, even as the apple seed is transformed in the red earth and the heathland is converted by the Spring.

You may have heard the tale of the man who saw the 'Reaper' gaping at him in one town and fled in terror to another town, only to meet the dreaded spectre there, at the 'appointed' time and place – the requisite homily about Fate unbending!

But you have not been told of the master who could *send* that spectre *away*, bidding him return at a time of the master's own choosing. Yeah, in this untold tale, the 'Reaper' recoils, abashed, like an overzealous boy who had jumped the queue or like a servant who, anxious to please, had shot forth from his lord's audience before he could wholly grasp the command!

And you may not have been told of the *grand* master who would surrender the soul to none but the Parent of all breaths and the Writer of the first Covenant, needing no go-between and trusting none other than the First Author.

And yet, even as I speak, many a dance in which Life and death join hands in mutual faith and festivity is kneading the earth into new seasons.

Your mentor will tell you that as a believer in Life you will deem each day a gift and every labour a blessing and a trust.

He will point out Life's altars in the world, where you will place your offerings, even at the doorsteps of those who deem themselves your enemies. And once you have commended your fealty to Life you may not be disowned by her.

To your teacher you will be as a cosmic extension, and to you he will be as a cosmic mirror. And he will give you of the light that is in him to guide you to the light that is within you, on your journey to the larger Light.

Verily, when the mind of your mentor and your own mind flow together you will advance to the higher Mind as skilled dancers move towards the summit of their act.

And though you may see your master as the wing that raises you to the truth, he will see himself as a feather in a greater wing, even as every prophet knows himself to be a link in a greater chain and a paladin in a relentless procession.

Truly you may sit at the bank of your mentor's wisdom lifting to your mouth the sweet crystals of his learning. But *he* may wander on the hazy roads with madmen and dazed palmers baffled and intoxicated even as *they* are by the mystery of Life.

The parable has been told of the master who turned down a young applicant, only to see her walking away across a deep river, her head bowed down in grief, her feet barely touching the water!

Unimpeded like a forgotten hymn, your mentor will be the envoy of all those voices that would not be seized by tablet or parchment but would travel in silent song from mind to mind.

And as your master passes, he will leave in your soul a testimony that will not wane and a holy writ forever writing new words.

But pity the people who invest their destiny in one man and set him up as sole guide so that when he dies, crumbling into their hearts like a stricken mountain, they claw their cheeks and gash their eyes and bury themselves in his towering dust. Or they would stalk the pathways to murder those who say he was dead, deranged by the passing of his flame.

And yet a true messenger would have taught them, had they cared to listen with their innermost hearts, that they too were flames and would be fanned best, even to eternity, by the unfettered breeze.

And again he was astride the auburn horse whose eyes were like blazing wine, journeying upon the ocean back into the receding sun.

And as his vast seafaring ended, he came to a huge harbour and once again saw the copper woman shimmering high above the tethered ships.

And in the woman's metallic but brave and kindly face he saw the faces of many women. And she seemed to bend down and offer him a torch she was carrying.

And the torch blazed fiercely as he stretched his arm towards it almost scorching his face, the roaring heat causing him to shut his eyes. But when, in his rage to see, he forced his eyes open, his irises were seized by the sight of winged female beings arrayed round a now clement torch.

And one who had azure-blue eyes extended her arms outwards to him with a reassuring and confirming smile.

She was taller than the rest but less perfect in body, with a somewhat ungainly head and bird-like features.

His seeking self felt drawn to her. And as he drew nearer he brushed against the softness of the other female forms, which made him shudder. And he shut his eyes more yieldingly than before and turned in a gyre of intoxication. But he recovered and found his way to her, knowing she was his assigned guardian and disciple.

And she held out an arm to him and let her hand rest on his chest, where her fingers travelled as though reading some invisible runes etched in the skin. Then she let her other hand draw his face to her dainty bosom, which heaved and nestled against his temples like a cooing dove. And when she gave him her lips, he tasted anew the fire on the lips of the angel who had appeared to him on the white mountain. And he felt confirmed in his gift and calling, though he did not fully know why and for what purpose he was chosen, despite the fact he had long clamoured for a mission.

And she led him to a lake at whose bank she bent forward and dipped a finger in the water. And the water turned red, and she bade him enter it.

And he waded, soul-bare, into the lake, and she entered the water by his side. And the water became as brilliant as liquefied diamond.

And after she had led him out of the lake and clothed him in a rough woollen garment, which chafed at his neck, he looked back at the lake and it was dark as ebony; but stars were glittering in its surface, and the image of a little Book was floating among the alien lights.

And there was a dim cry, half-heard as though it came from afar but also from deep within the woman's soul. And she turned her face aside over her broad shoulder as if listening, unmoored from her closeness to him. And he felt a fount of sadness bubbling up inside him, but also a billowing relief.

Freedom, more festive than that promised by the

guardian's wings, embraced him, his own sinews hollering to be so cradled, and so extended.

And then a voice pulled him back to the people. An undertaker was saying, I am feared and shunned on the roads; and yet when their loved ones die, men come knocking on my door at the crack of dawn! What say you of funerals and burials?

And, he, buffeted by waves of keening and rejoicing ebbing and flowing within him, said:

As the winged caterpillar will abandon her old skin on the thistle, so will a man cast off his body, though often in pain and regret.

And he will seem to hover above it for an instant in wonder and vague sympathy.

But the body deserves respect, even though it can no more count the rosary of its days or circle the hallowed shrine.

It is then that the living shall pay their homage to the mystery of Life by honouring one of her nightingales who has moved deeper into the star-lidded forest.

And it will be a thanksgiving for the song which will abide, and for the music maker.

And as the priest will speak of how the melodies of the migrant bird touched the lives of those gathered together, he will remind them of the duty of singing and of the notes that linger upon the branches and mingle with the constellations.

And yet there will be those at the service who will glance furtively at the hurrying sun and are anxious to get back to their fields and to their shops.

And that is not always hard-hearted, for Life does not stand still, nor will she be cast into one mould.

But even for those whose minds are set on buying and selling or are restless to return to the bracing chorus of their children's voices, the ceremony of parting will instil in them some tenderness and move them to reflection.

And for those whose hearts are too frail for thoughts of death and suffering, that same ceremony may give them needed strength and insight. For they too shall one day travel into the forest as their bodies are borne on the shoulders of men. And they must be prepared for that hour without snubbing the days and nights that pour into their hands Life's rubies and sapphires and amethysts.

Often we hear of people journeying forth. And we are bewildered and aggrieved. But seldom do we see ourselves in the bier. And that again is a glimpse of Life's sacred cunning.

And though the shared farewell is meant to soothe and sustain, a funeral solely decreed by custom and the need for show may distance us further from the dead. And when the ritual is done and the undertakers paid, we will be prevailed upon to sweep the dark garments from our shoulders and the ash from our hearts. Before long, the counsellors will call the deceased a weight removed and the thought of death a jeopardy.

The honey of such advice is sweet, but there is a sting floating in the golden nectar.

For it is seemly to reflect back on roads travelled and summits scaled, aye, even as we pledge our eyes to the horizon. And as faith and prayer need no temple, and surely no pastor, so can the heart alone, with its plainness and silence, be the shrine where the ceremony of parting is enacted.

But the heart, that small cup which can hold all the dew of the universe, shall not be a tomb.

From it there will flow eternal the sweet, stubborn stream of Life.

Verily, there will always be unease between the gravity of ritual and the surges of the human heart. But there may also be a partnership! And behind a hearse carried on the marrow of men a nation may become whole.

But woe to the priest refusing burial to a rebel who rose up against the stern temple or to a woman who flew her cage and poured forth her song in the free air or to a pauper who sought his gold among the leaves of the beech and the dimples of the setting sun! For, until these stretch their hands to him from the depths of the Wood with the grace and clemency of the enlightened, he will confound his entry into the greater Mercy.

So deem not the pall a curtain and the spade a seal, but rather a standard and a spur plunging us more deeply into the greater Mind.

Brief will be the prickle of death; a little shiver in the nippy air, and the arrow will leap forth, no more chafed by the string.

A small flutter, a slight froth, and the awkward, lumbering fowl shall glide upon the river – a regal Swan! A moment's sojourn in the dark chamber and the silkworm shall bask in the sun and soar above the shroud, a Monarch!

And an apprentice astronomer asked, What say you of the vastness and silence of space? Its aimlessness and indifference strike

fear in many a heart. Might life be no more than a spawn of that pointlessness, a speck of that Oblivion, that horror?

And Almustafa raised his gaze heavenwards then lowered it into his heart. He sought out the Stalker to challenge him to another duel; so confident was he in his peace! But he suddenly felt like a boy running around with a toy sword, and he grimaced in embarrassment and shame. Anon, he tore his gaze away, and answered the young man saying:

If the learned say that we came from Nothing, then we should not fear returning to it since it is the very essence and fabric of our being. In truth, some may see in this a benefit and a rest eternal. They may praise this circumstance, where Permanence is a dead tyrant and the embrace of Oblivion a happy release, the crowning of Man's doom-bound journey.

I will not call this philosophy blasphemous, for there is courage in it, and compassion for a humanity often conned by false promises and hobbled by fears of unnatural tortures in an invented underworld.

But might it be that Oblivion was the very bag out of which God pulled the miracle of creation, and is thus a testimony to celestial magic – and to the power and prudence of the celestial Mage? Might it be a loving challenge to Man to be God-like, replicating the act of creation and dotting the bleak silences with brilliance and song?

I would bless the void, the empty purse from which came the wealth, and the fearsome beauty, of the stars and the forests and the oceans.

And I would bless the vastness of space, for it is both a banquet ever spreading and a shade that guards many an apprenticed eye from too much radiance.

And yet it is also a mirror of the vastness within, and of the vastness struggling to come forth; and it is also an invitation.

There, in the streaming sanctum, perform your ablutions and dedicate your hymns, even as they stumble over their notes, to the miracle of Life and all her quarrelling children.

It is also in the infinite fields that your acts, even your thoughts, shall bud and bear fruit. And from the harps of their branches shall you send the melodies that will make men and angels swoon with wonder.

For what is an albatross without his un-bounded sky, even with his tireless wings?

Verily, you shall need all that vastness to

scatter the seeds of your compassion and acknowledge the compassion of others. And in it you shall meet the souls you have known and those you wished to know, and with whom you shall dance to ecstasy.

And is not the sigh of the lover, baffled and distraught by the immensity of his passion, dearer to God than the grin of the miser counting his coins?

And would you not cast your treasure to the stream of stars rather than hoard it for the tomb robber?

And a philosopher reasoned, Is not the fear of death a mark of a sensitive soul, for surely it is a callous and coarse man who does not know fear?

And Almustafa replied, and there was a nettle struggling to blossom in his voice:

Truly, the path of one who serenades 'Wisdom' can lead him under intriguing balconies!

But fear, lingering, is a seasoned trickster. He ingratiates himself to us as an angel only to turn into a demon within. Ever a schemer, he whispers tales of fellowship and the hearth, but spirits his claws into our heart to lacerate its greater yearnings and spill its star-blood.

Fear, abiding, is the dodder stem that coils,

ravenous, round our expanding self; the sly cuckoo whose brood will shove our own into the chasm. He is the despotic tradition that crushes our dancer-feet in an ambrosial vault; the thorn under the saddle that drives our mustang mad.

Time and again the merchant has used the fear of death to draw our purses to his gimmick; and the priest has used it to bind our souls to his beads, and the tyrant to bend our nobility to his vulgar will.

The generals planning the moves of their pawn-soldiers on the dusty board are but themselves pawns in the terrible game. Even the jilted lover who climbs the high cliff to dash his anguish onto the rocks below is but one similarly trapped.

Some may praise this fear as the string that sends the spinning top a-whirl or the spark that gives the lamp its night-dispersing glow.

But when we wear the shirt of fear, perpetual, we are likely to wear underneath it the vest of hate. And though they may not know it, the planters and weavers of terror will themselves (or their own children) don its spikes and drink its poison.

Part of our fear of death is the fear of the

dark and solitude. But wombs – who does not know? – bring forth infant joys as nebulae stars. And in the red earth the rainbow sets its many-coloured roots and the festival of rebirth is ever astir.

Ho! Hearken to the joy of the hawk flying away from his hood! And, Ah, see him return to the King's arm!

And this I say also, though it may hurt in the telling. The gentle saint on her Cross may bless her murderers who have helped her rise, body and soul, to her great Lover, who, because of his greater love cannot but be the greater Sufferer.

But it is Life that the saint and other defeaters of terror serve and adorn. This they do so we may see with Life's eyes and walk with her feet and touch the eager petals with her sacred hands.

For to foil the ogres that lurk for him on his journey, a man will need to take them into his own, thereby transforming their bile into sweetness and their sickness into wholesome growth, aye even their stealth into courage and their frenzy into endurance. This will be his elevation and his triumph.

But such a man will not be boastful; nor will he hide behind a shield of indifference or fear.

Trust ye that even when fear staggers from

the dark corner to stop the rush of stars, the light *shall* prevail. And will not, in the arms of death, the terror of a thousand ills and a thousand alarms dissolve into an irrelevance? And might not the suspended sword melt into a mist, perhaps a halo? Might it not?

O my fear, my crafty fear, will *you* not rise from the shadows and barter your bat's wing for an astral plume?

And an old sculptor pleaded, Would you speak to us of the numberless deaths poets have not sung and for whom carvers have cut no headstones?

And he, remembering his own labours with the hardness of words and the dread of a life without a name or mission, answered saying:

In the fields and wastelands of the world and amongst seaweeds and on riverbeds, and at the crossroads of war-chariots and below the palaces of kings, lie the bones of those who fell by the blows of human confusion.

And beneath the dust of the busy roads and under the bracken and avens of the mountain-sides rest the mortal remains of women and men who sought bread for their children or aspired to breathe a fresher air and revive their hearts in the cold mist.

They lie in unmarked graves and no lines or laurels are given them by the official histories, cluttered as these are with the pageantries of conquerors and kings.

Yea, the nameless fallen are deemed mere chaff of the processions filing from humble hearths and fettered fields, trudging along history's roadsides. A humdrum fate that makes the boy in the old tale choose to live a brief but 'glorious' life instead of a long and un-remembered one!

But in the Book of the Universe all the deeds are set down, and all the words, spoken and hushed, are heeded.

Nor will the legacy of a man come to an end when he is laid to rest in his grave.

For the seeds that he planted will surely grow in the sun. And as long as these continue to give shade and fruit, and the seeds of that fruit give unto the seasons, he shall live on earth and his name shall scintillate in the fields of light and be praised by the mysterious choirs of Life.

And even if the green beings he planted were to be uprooted by axe or gale, they shall continue to blossom and yield fruit in other worlds, and there too his name shall be honoured.

And through the lives of the men and women the damned deserter has spared by casting his sword away, *he* too shall continue to live. *Their* children and grandchildren will be as his own. And though they may not learn of him or of his charity, their own good deeds and offerings shall, unbeknown to them, enhance his chronicle in the Book.

Truly, the wise find words on tombstones a trifling, for they can easily grasp the eloquence of the moss-grown mound and the cracked marble. And it is within their means to scan the music of the desert wind and read the runes of the desolate coast. And from the waves and pebbles they can well hear the requiems and carols of endless renewal and feel the ripples of Life's web humming within their hearts!

And as the night breeze carries the breath of the hidden rose to forlorn windows so will the un-chronicled acts of the Life-dedicated souls find their way to our depths. And so will they startle us into wonder and expectation, even as a May's mate-seeking wagtail turns his head towards a rustle in the distance, his heart a-leap.

Truly, the very air we breathe is a spirit-repository, and the earth a coffer and a highway. And as we ascend a path worn smooth for our climb, we shall bless all the feet that have helped our pilgrimage to the holy cedars.

And let me whisper this in your ears — perchance it may soothe mine! No *true* pilgrim will trek to a warlord's castle or offer his devotion to glowering parapets. Rather, he will walk across glens and gullies seeking the fragrance of hermits and saints, prophets and lovers, who joyfully unravelled their bodies on the earth's loom and their voices to the wind's abandon, there to bask in their subtle exuberance.

And a politician asked, and what of a larger death, that of a nation?

And he answered:

A nation will fall, often by her own hand, long before a foreign army had breached her walls.

But the most galling end of a nation is when she loses her soul in the clutter of possessions.

For a nation shall wither away, even like a chrysanthemum in Ielul, when she swells with self-importance and when her high-mindedness stifles her humility, and when she can no longer laugh with her children or at her own foolery.

And a nation shall stiffen as a corpse when she

fails to give from her heart and basket to other nations. For how can Life *be* without giving!

It is a grim fate for a river to turn into a bog, dense with smug reflections and dark dreams. Better for him to pour his liquid soul into a boundless desert and perish gasping on the blistering sands! A river fulfils his destiny when he rushes along his hard-won course, turning the mills and watering the farms on his way to the great sea. The large boulders and the sheer falls in his path will be as pebbles and merry slides compared to the dour brooding of the swamp.

And a nation is deemed to be no more with the living when she frequents the gilded mausoleums of her past and shuns the hovels of her present; and when she squanders her wealth on studded spears only to beg her conquerors for jewelled carriages. Aye, and when she holds the cloaked casements a virtue and the free-born word a menace and a heresy.

Never will a good nation be crushed from without. For, even as her temples and vineyards, and gardens and libraries, are ravaged and her defenders mowed down, she will live through her wandering minstrels and exiled prophets. And with their time-riding rhymes

and prophecies she may lead on the distant horizons a worthier life and spread a larger banquet. Aye, even as the lotus seed may be carried down the river to flourish in hallowed licence by the temple's side, and as the orchid bud is lifted by the wind to the towering tree, and as the people trodden underfoot by conquerors and persecutors turn into the elysian wine of the world and a deliverance unto it.

Even when all her scrolls and songs and children are reduced to dust, the nation will live, be it as a faint sermon and a flickering gleam, in the memories of other nations, even as the throats and wings and passions of long-lost birds live in those of the kingfisher and the hoopoe and the nightingale.

But, death, my friends, is not a failure.

And for those who happen to be breathing the air when their nation is dying, they must not despair. For it may be that at the birth of a nation the air is too giddy, and at the height of her power the air is too settled. Perhaps a gentle and thoughtful air will linger when a nation is dying –

Dying, perchance, to rise again, like a Phoenix!

And now the mist returned in strength to

Almustafa's eyes, and both his hands came up to savour it, even as the people surged towards him only to withdraw to some distance like a tide retreating or a suitor abashed.

And Almustafa stood alone with both hands over his eyes. And his hands sought the mist even as the mist sought his hands and the core of his being; yet he was loath to abandon the anxious crowd pulsating at bay.

And as before, he was himself of a former day, released from his guardian angel, journeying into many selves as human as he was, ministering to them from his visions and cravings while being nourished and validated by their own imaginings and needs. His confidence was growing, sprouting new plumes and melodies. And he was braced by his human fellowships as he tended to the quarrelling beliefs ministering to them by the glad impulse of the universe in him. Even then, he was hammering now and again on a colossal door, which continued to tantalise him with glimpses of concealed wonders and echoes of seraphic wisdom and the rustling of innumerable wings.

But, he was increasingly being aware of the vagueness and contradictions of his own self – even of its smallness and brittleness, and of its bottomless greed.

And he felt a tightness in his chest as he dared the words of his little Book to burgeon into leaves and for these leaves to girdle the world like a sash about the waist of a dancer. And he willed them to enfold the world as the wings of a dove or an eagle might enfold their hatchlings but then to seize like a titan the chains forged by pashas and priests and politicians and tear them apart as frivolous chimeras.

But as he scoured the far-flung woods and galleries he could only see leaves stillborn in their sheaths on stunted albino trees, and drawings of beings with angels' wings and goats' hooves hung forlornly on walls with peeling paint. And he could only see men with vulture faces squatting outside his childhood home on the white mountain, their claw-like hands clutching pages from his Book hoping, as though outside a treasury, to convert them into pieces of gold and silver. And he saw others posing as educators and reviewers mocking his Book and disgorging their jealousies and spite unto its pages, upon which they crawled like scorpions with their frantic litter on their backs. And over the lanes and hills and highroads he saw spectral fetters loosening only to engulf more and more people and drive them implacably in vagrant and factious directions, even as the folk carolled and cheered in their wretched march.

And he sought to cling in his fear and desperation

to the selves through whose depths he had been tunnelling and quarrying, perhaps betraying, plundering, and to the voices in the wind he had been stalking and the visions of angels which his lust for life had invoked. A searing lament burned in his heart, and a mocking requiem of his mission (his mission?) boomed in his ears.

And he felt intense shame at his own inadequacy and at the pretences of his calling. His knocking on the ineffable, tantalizing, door and on many lesser, earthly, portals rang too loudly and hollowly in his head, and he sensed too keenly the waywardness of his motives and the futility of his labours, leaf-bound and patch-freckled, amidst the enormity of emptiness and the endlessness of discord.

And he burst into a great sob which seemed to consume his whole being.

And in the vastness of his despair he sought in the leaps and loops of time the winged patroness of his earlier vision. And he saw her shorn of her wings, wandering in a curdled mist with dishevelled grey hair and a vacant look in her faded blue eyes. And he passed by another woman from the isle of his birth with whom he had shared a song of freedom but was now strapped by her own kinsmen to a narrow bed as she lay dying on it in manacled rage. And he saw another and another whose glowing bodies he had

embraced and whose soaring souls he had chaperoned;
he saw them bloating and shrivelling in weed-gutted
gardens and doleful rooms.

And he saw a ring of fire surrounding the white
mountain of his native land and causing the snow
on its summit to melt. And he saw men with
hissing torches setting alight the body of a dead
man who had his face. And he saw other torches in
contracted hands drifting as though on bat-like
wings. He saw them setting fire to hamlet after
hamlet and field after field, fanning dark flames in
the hearts of onlookers. Soon the melted snow was
rushing down the mountainside in crimson cascades,
which then leapt and bounced over the pebbles and
shells of the shore and began to tinge the sea with a
sickly flush.

And a thought suggested to him that the Stalker
was in truth unvanquished and on the verge of
claiming his soul and hauling it into the vast void,
consigning his labours to the realms of futility and
ridicule. And in his desolation and pain he was
about to hurl a curse at the absence of God and the
dimming of the joy he had sought so stubbornly to
earn and share when a Woman's chant per-
colated through the turbid maelstrom of his
doubts and denials. And he felt his head reclining
on a soft thigh and himself looking up into the

hazel eyes of his Mother as she sang him an ancient lullaby.

Beyond the gauze scarf that lay lightly like a halo on her head, great pendant stars were crowding the deep-blue night sky, attending on the Woman's tender omnipotence. And the stars shone so near that he reached up with his right hand to pluck one of them, feigning, as when a child, to place it under his pillow when he went to sleep.

And he felt the warmth of the star pulsating in the palm of his hand, and its light radiating through his sinking body, healing its qualms and welding together the vagrant and battling strands of his life and quests into meaning and triumph. The ending, he knew beyond doubt, was a beginning, a continual embrace, a revelation and a salutation rather than a shunning and a shutting down.

He made a last physical effort and strained his head to look into the light of the star in his palm from which now shone the Woman's face even as he feebly beckoned to invite the people into his last vision. And he died with a wonder in his eyes and theirs and a blessing twitching on his lips and soaring from their own.

*   *   *

And all the people of Orphalese came together to mourn and bid him farewell. And though they would have his body interred in their own earth, to raise for him a shrine there, some of his disciples maintained that Almustafa's native soil was a more fitting urn for the deserted hull of his breath.

Almitra, who had journeyed in her anguish to the city and kept a vigil beside the dead master, held that the dust of his adopted land was as holy a sepulchre as that which echoed to his youthful footfalls.

And she argued that shackling Almustafa to the isle of his birth was a betrayal of his universal mission and ever-pilgrim words.

But her voice did not prevail.

On a misty morn, as the sunflowers were lifting their heads towards a diffident sun, the body of Almustafa was borne from the temple and taken to the harbour. There, a ship with a white and red flag drooping from the top of her mast waited in the low tide.

And a great cry of pain rose from the multitude of mourners on the quay as the coffin passed, carried on to the deck of the ship by six disciples.

And as the ship sailed into the slowly

climbing sun, Almitra followed her with tearful eyes and a tremulous prayer until the vessel disappeared into the haze.

In the course of time, the ship dropped anchor in the harbour of Almustafa's home isle. There, a large crowd had gathered, having received reports of the coming of the ship and of the great grieving and reverence that had attended the exile's passing in distant Orphalese.

The bells tolled in the island's towers and invocations streamed from its tapering columns as the hearse was brought out of the ship's bowels. The prince of the land, who in the past had been counselled to fear Almustafa's mission, was at the pier flanked by glittering courtiers and decorated generals; and they all bowed in studied deference before the coffin. And the clerics, who had declared Almustafa a heretic and a sham, swayed their censers chanting well-rehearsed prayers for the dead.

And all along the road to Almustafa's birth-place in the sacred Mount, the common people, unbound for the day from their lords, came out of their stone houses and terraced fields to pay homage and live a dream of freedom.

This was their own son, whose very sinews

had been chiselled by their rugged Mountain and honed to keenness by the air they inhaled; but, he, alone, had the daring to awaken the dormant fire in the rock and waft it into light and joy for their cold and cheerless nights.

Strange and stirring reports of him had travelled from across the ocean into their solemn abodes, even against the hissing of the priest and the bellowing of the pasha. They had travelled, not like the fumes of the sly weed to dull the mind with false visions, but like the orisons of a rare and irrepressible songbird, unfettered and fearless.

But now they were stricken, bereft of him in mid-flight. And yet as they lingered, dazed and sluggish, on the mountain slopes, their souls soared with the converging pinions of a stubborn dream.

Young men, wearing belts of many-layered native silk, engaged in swordplay in an ancient form of tribute to a fallen hero. Poets read out elegies, and old women chanted lamentations and beat their dried up breasts in tune with their chanting. Fair maidens, tears a-sparkle in their gazelle eyes, loosened their long raven braids and sprinkled rose petals and orange-blossom water on the slowly moving cortege, all the while singing in welcome of the bride-groom and homecoming.

And in a chapel of an ancient monastery on the sheer face of a gorge not far from the eternally white summit, they laid him in a little crypt. This was a place he loved in his youth and often visited to wait, clamouring, for the angels. The monastery, a little fortress of the spirit hewn out of the mountainside, had echoed to the chants of countless creeds. The timeless cedars girdling it had lent their precious wood to many altars and icons, and myriad hearts had been warmed and chilled by the crag martins that chirped past it in summer and the winds that howled about it in winter.

And to this crypt pilgrims came and knelt before the casket, lighting candles with doting fingers and invoking Almustafa's deathless ardour for life to intercede in trysts and marriages, even in the prayer for a miracle to visit a barren womb. Supplicants with wider worries and bolder hopes prayed for a nation marooned and a world adrift. Poets and sculptors solicited wings for their words and sparks for their stone, though also petitioning these, as Almustafa had urged, within their own souls. Outside, traders peddled relics made from cedar wood and seashells, even from the fibre of Almustafa's childhood garments. Rich and powerful men vied to establish themselves as sole custodians of the traffic in Almustafa's freely given wisdom.

In time, when men fought amongst one another for control of these transactions, a group of them, deranged by the loss of their franchise, vowed to deny the resource to all. One sent to torch the body in the hallowed casket however emerged a changed man. He was to shed the last embers of his fury in the caves of the heights as a hermit, while the country below him convulsed in a wider conflagration for few more years.

Still every Spring, pilgrims wind their way over the craggy slopes of the holy Mount, past the bouncing icy streamlets of melted snow and the tenacious pine and thuya trees, towards the austere shrine perched beneath a dwindling clump of ageing cedars. There they see, flickering and fluttering in the crisp breeze, the reddest and liveliest anemones and crowfoots ever seen anywhere else.

On some special nights, it is rumoured, the pilgrim keeping vigil outside the crypt is rewarded with a strange experience, during which a woman's voice suddenly issues from the vast darkness singing a lullaby to a child. When this happens, unnerving the faint-hearted, the woman is answered by a mysterious songbird whom none can relate to any known bird species. His notes, it is said, will clamour relentlessly under the diminishing starlight until they dissolve into a choir of skylarks, wheatears, sparrows, and serins celebrating the flame of a new day.

ACKNOWLEDGEMENTS

The above narrative, in its felicitous intervals, owes a debt to many. Besides Gibran himself, who, in contrast to some other school material, was a living and ever-relevant subject to us as schoolchildren in Lebanon, I may mention:

My mother, Isaaf, for her extraordinary gentleness and fear of all partings but unfaltering courage in defence of her children and students and all children and students of life;

My father, Atef, for his humaneness and liberal and liberating parenting and for his phenomenal fearlessness at all times. The trip he organised for his young family, my mother, sister, brother, and myself, to Bisharri when I was only seven was my first real introduction to Gibran and remains a vivid and moving memory;

Suheil Bushrui for his pioneering and inspirational AUB course on Gibran and other Lebanese writers in America, and for his painstaking but ever-radiant writings and campaigns to place Gibran within the canon of great writers, to whom he too should belong;

The late Ernest Becker for his stirring study *The Denial of Death*, which was the first book I bought when I came to Cambridge from war-torn Beirut through Oxford in 1976;

Helen and James Kinnier Wilson and Ranam Al Ghazzi to whom I read out the first draft of this text and received their inestimable and typically unstinting encouragement and astute advice;

The spiritual and mystical traditions of all faiths as they celebrate life and continuity, courage and unity, hope and peace for all – a tradition perhaps summed up beautifully though never exclusively or finally in the works and lives of luminaries like Rab'ia, 'Attar, Ibn 'Arabi, Ibn Gabirol, Rumi, Teresa of Avila, Blake, and Tagore;

Lebanon, with all her teachers, poets, artists, lovers, diplomats, and ordinary/extraordinary people and her beautiful mountain villages, where everyone is a Messenger, a mediator between the ineffable and the expressible, and each one is a Prophet of a new dawn;

The people of America who have given Gibran so much from the expansiveness of their land and the durability and richness of their faith and imagination;

Finally, to Naim Attallah this book owes the singular gratitude of being taken from a tedious antechamber to a reception hall ever animated by Naim's liberality and brilliance. At Quartet Books, David Elliott's exceptional patience and editorial acumen I acknowledge with deep appreciation.

A SELECT BIBLIOGRAPHY

Bushrui, Suheil and Munro, John M. (eds), *Kahlil Gibran: Essays and Introductions*, Beirut, Rihani House, 1970

Bushrui, Suheil and Gotch, Paul, (eds), *Gibran of Lebanon: New Papers,* Beirut, Librairie du Liban, 1975

Bushrui, Suheil, *Kahlil Gibran of Lebanon: A Reevaluation of the Author of 'The Prophet',* Gerrards Cross, Colin Smythe, 1987

Bushrui, Suheil and Salma al-Kuzbari, (trans and eds), *Gibran: Love Letters,* Oxford, OneWorld Publications, 1995

Bushrui, Suheil and Jenkins, Joe, *Kahlil Gibran: Man and Poet – A New Biography,* Oxford, OneWorld Publications, 1998

Gibran, Kahlil, *The Prophet,* introduction and annotations by Suheil Bushrui, Oxford, OneWorld Publications, 1995

Gibran, Kahlil and Gibran, Jean, *Kahlil Gibran: His Life and World,* New York, Interlink Books, 1991

Naimy, Mikhail, *Kahlil Gibran: His Life and His Work,* Beirut, Khayats, 1965

Otto, A. S. (ed.), *The Letters of Kahlil Gibran and Mary Haskell,* Houston, 1967

Young, Barbara, *This Man from Lebanon: A Study of Kahlil Gibran,* New York, 1956